I0518655

Four Faces of Death

Other Books By
A. H. Holt

Fiction

High Plains Fort
Ten in Texas
Silver Creek
Blanco Sol
Riding Fence
Kendrick
Blood Redemption
XIT Ranch
The Malefactors

Nonfiction

Grant Writing Step by Step
From Writer to Author
Beautiful Places:
Monticello & Jefferson County Florida

Four Faces of Death
By A. H. Holt

© Copyright 2017 by A. H. Holt
All rights reserved.
All the characters in this book are fictitious,
and any resemblance to actual persons,
living or dead, is purely coincidental.

ISBN: 9780998387710
ASIN: B0722NWGXG

Dedicated to
Bettie and Zoe.
My Beautiful Great Grand Daughters.

FOUR FACES OF DEATH

Quiet Revenge
A Touch of Love
Goodbye
A New Ending

Quiet Revenge

Beyond a Shadow of a Doubt

Rafe settled closer to the trunk of the big live oak and eased the rifle out over a limb as he watched the man approaching along the edge of the creek. Tall and thin, the man held his head down as he watched the path, whistling softly.

Shifting slightly, Rafe leveled his rifle with the man's chest and whispered, "Come on you son-of-a-bitch, come on." The man walked to a thicket of elders near the road and reached down to fumble around in the brush a moment. Looking puzzled, he stood up with his hands on his hips, looking around.

Rafe smiled and held his breath as he aimed at the top pocket on the man's blue jacket. The crack of the rifle sent crows squalling up out of the brush. He could hear the jangle of metal on his horse's bridle as the animal jerked his head in alarm.

The front of his jacket streaked with blood, the man flopped to the ground without a sound. Rafe ducked under the limb and walked closer to stand over the body. Reaching down, he caught the man's left shoulder and yanked him up away from the ground to look at his back. A ragged hole gaped where the heavy bullet exited.

Rafe spoke aloud, as though the dead man could hear his words. "I reckon you won't run after no other man's wife, damn your sorry hide."

Dropping the rifle beside the body, Rafe yanked off his leather gloves and stuffed them in the pocket of his duster. He went back to the tree where he waited and retrieved his own rifle from the ground, turned away from the creek, and pushed through the line of hackberry bushes to his horse. Mounting quickly, he turned the roan south along the faint trail.

Rafe came out of the woods at MacQueen's store and post office, the only building still standing in what early settlers once hoped might be the town of Bartonsville.

He yelled to the man sitting on the porch. "Hey, Mac, I need your help."

"What the devil's the matter Rafe?" MacQueen jumped up from his chair and walked to the edge of the porch.

Rafe dismounted and carefully tied his horse's reins to the hitching post. Walking up the steps, he leaned one hand against a porch post and said, "I better sit down here alongside you for a minute, Mac. I sorta need to get my breath."

"Take this chair, Rafe—you trying to kill that horse of yours? He looks like you run him all the way from your place, boy. Is Ellie sick?"

"No-no-it ain't that." Rafe held up one hand. "I found Lin Richardson shot, down by Taylor's Creek."

MacQueen's mouth hung open for a second, then he gasped, "Gosh almighty, is he dead?"

"He's got a hole in his back big as my hand. He's dead all right. Mac, send your boy up to the courthouse and get Sonny Martin down here."

"Heck yes. You come on inside the store and get yourself a drink of cool water, son. You look all done up."

Rafe drank a dipper of water from the bucket hanging just inside the door and wiped his face on the arm of his coat.

Walking to the back of the store, he leaned against the counter to fish in his jeans pocket for a coin. Slapping it down on the counter, he said, "Pour me a drink out of that bottle you keep hid, Mac. I'm feeling plumb unnerved."

Rafe picked up his drink and moved to a group of chairs near the stove to sit down in the one nearest the counter. Keeping his head low, he watched and listened as MacQueen stuck his head in the door of his living quarters at the back of the store, called his son Eddie and ordered him to ride for the sheriff.

When the wide-eyed boy rushed out of the store, MacQueen returned to lean over the counter. "Who do you reckon got Lin, Rafe?"

"Shucks Mac, it could have been half a dozen guys. Lin didn't have no shame a'tall about sneaking around another man's wife. That is—if talk can be believed."

"He was a rounder, that's for sure. You heard any talk about who he was running after lately?"

Rafe kept his eyes down as he took another sip of his drink before he answered. "Mac, you know I ain't had me no use for Lin Richardson since he got smart with my Ellie at the yearling sale last year. Folks plumb quit talking about him around me."

"Well I can't say I blame you for that. Been a time, any sorry bastard messed with my Mary better hada stayed clear of me."

Rafe stood up to stretch and walked over to look out the front door. "How long you reckon it'll take for Sonny to get down here?"

"Oh, about a hour, I'd say – maybe more. Sonny's never been known to be quick about anything."

Mac leaned over counter with his chin on his hands. His pale eyes didn't meet Rafe's. "How'd you come to find Lin, Rafe?"

Rafe tensed and took the time to walk back to his seat near the stove before answering. "I rode up beside Taylor's creek on my way over to Nelson Lewis' place and there he was, flat on the ground. You recollect where that crooked road used to go across the creek near the old Parrish place?"

"Yeah, I know where you mean, the road comes out about at that big sycamore by Bob Jackson's farm."

"You're right—that's exactly where I mean. Lin was right there in a bunch of vines—on the edge of the creek-- not in the water or anything, but just off the path. My horse didn't like the smell of blood, so I got down and went over to check on him. That's some nasty hole in his back. I'll wager he died before he hit the ground."

MacQueen shook his head as if he couldn't believe what he was hearing. "Ain't that something? Nothing like this has happened in this county since them Anthonys got shot over to Billy Nowell's place back in seventy-one. I reckon you remember. Folks talked about that for a spell."

Rafe shook his head, his expression almost sad. "It'll be a nine-days wonder, that's for sure."

The pounding of horses' hooves preceded the sheriff into the store yard. Sonny Martin jumped from his saddle, dropping his horse's reins to the ground and bounded up the steps.

"Mac, you close up and come go with Rafe and me down to the creek." His voice was too loud and painfully high-pitched.

"You go to hell, Sonny Martin." Mac said with a frown as he straightened up from the counter. "I ain't tramping the woods for you or nobody else—do your own dirty work."

"Aw Mac, don't be so dammed touchy. Me and Rafe are gonna need some help packing Lin's body out of the woods. You know that."

"Well my advice is to go around by way of Bob Jackson's place to get over there. He's got a slew of big boys that can help you haul Lin out. Seeing as how you came out here on horseback, he'll have a buckboard you can borrow to haul the body back to town."

"I met your boy half-way here. How do you think I got here so fast? I was heading to Jake Davis' place about that still of his. He claims to have quit making, but folks are still going around with shine in them tall quart jars he always uses.

"That's good thinking about borrowing a buckboard from Bob Jackson though, Mac. I'll just do that. You ready to go, Rafe?"

Rafe stood up and stretched. "I'm ready Sonny. Let's get this thing done."

As he ran down the steps ahead of Rafe, Sonny shouted over his shoulder, "You can tell me about it while we ride."

Rafe mounted and rode alongside Sonny. "There ain't much I can tell you, Sonny. I was coming up Taylor's creek from my place and found Lin's body lying on the ground beside the creek. It looks to me like he was shot with a Sharps hunting rifle from the size of the hole in him. His own Sharps lay there on the ground, right alongside him."

"You hadn't seen him before? Today, I mean?"

"I'd a told you if I had, Sonny." Rafe caught Sonny's eyes with his and looked grim.

"Now, don't get touchy, Rafe. I got my job to do."

His face red, Sonny urged his horse to a canter, leaving Rafe's horse a few yards behind. After a few minutes, he slowed down to let Rafe catch up again.

"You know I didn't mean nothing by what I said, Rafe."

"I know you've got a job to do, Sonny. I knew good and well I was in for some grief when I saw Lin's body lying there, but you can't just leave a man lying dead in the woods like that, it ain't Christian."

"Well, of course you had to tell somebody and send for me, Rafe seeing you found Lin's body like that. I'm obliged to you for it."

The men rode several miles without speaking. When they approached a small hill, Rafe said, "We can turn left up here at that half-dead sycamore tree and take the old road over to Bob Jackson's place. That old road's good enough for us on horseback and a heck of a lot shorter, but you'll have to bring the buckboard out the long way."

Bobby Jr. and Will Jackson eagerly agreed to help recover Lin's body. Will, the largest and obviously the eldest of the boys said, "Pa's done gone over to Hiltonville to fetch some grain in the buckboard, Sheriff. We got us a extry saddle horse though. That'll do for hauling a body.

"I'll put a saddle on the horse so's you'll have something to tie the man to. You don't want him falling off in the dirt on the way. You can get the horse back to us next passing."

Will and Bobby Jr. saddled their horses and leading the third horse with stirrups flapping on the empty saddle, rode close behind Rafe and Sonny, full of talk about who might have wanted to kill Lin Richardson.

The group cut across a field about a half mile from the farm house and followed Rafe along the old rutted road.

"Don't step near the body, you boys," Sonny ordered. "There might be evidence like tracks or some such."

Rafe stood back and watched as Sonny checked Lin's body. The Sheriff lifted the rifle from the ground beside the body, held it near his face and sniffed.

"This here gun's been fired."

Rafe smiled behind his hand. "Well, it sure don't look to me like Lin could have shot himself like that."

"There's no telling about something like that just by looking. We'll just have to take everything to Doc Daniel and let him study on it. He'll figure it out."

Sonny walked around the area half-heartedly looking for tracks. "I can't see no tracks that look strange, can you Rafe?"

"I ain't seen nothing but what you see, Sonny. I was on my way over to Nelson's to borrow a froe to fix the roof on my tool shed. He's about the only body left in the country that's got one. I rode right along the path there just like I always do and found Lin lying exactly the way you see him."

"Where was you when you heard the shot?"

"I never told you I heard no shot, Sonny Martin. It must a happened when I was milking or something. I never heard anything."

Sonny looked at Rafe intently. "I kind of find that surprising don't you—I mean that you wouldn't a heard the shot?"

Rafe stood up straight, the heavy rifle cradled in his arms, his face grim. "Are you trying to say something, Sonny?"

"Lord no, Rafe. Heck no. I told you before—I ain't in no way accusing you of anything. I'm just trying to figure this thing out."

"Well, maybe you could start to figure some other way. You're about to make me mad the way you're talking."

"Shucks, Rafe, nobody would think you're dumb enough to do this thing right on your own door step and then come running for me."

"I should hope folks would figure me better than that. Besides, my gun ain't been fired since it was cleaned. You can check it if you want to." With one swift motion, Rafe yanked his rifle around and held it almost in Sonny's face.

"I ain't interested, Rafe."

His face flushed, Sonny waved one hand and turned away. "Let's get that body out of here and quit jawing about it."

Careful to keep from touching the blood on Martin's jacket, Rafe and the Jackson boys helped Sonny carry Richardson's body to the horse, settle it over the saddle and tie it in place.

Stopping Sonny with one hand on his arm before he mounted to leave, Rafe asked, "Do I have to come to the courthouse about this mess?"

"No man, you done your duty. Let the Doc Daniels figure it out. He got appointed corner. I'll bet you a double eagle it's murder by persons unknown and that'll be the end of it."

"You let me know, will you Sonny? I'd take it as a favor."

"Sure I will, Rafe. I'll send word down to Mac's place soon's as I know anything, and thanks, boy."

Rafe waved his hand and walked back to his roan. Mounting, he followed the edge of the creek, taking ten minutes at a fast trot to reach his gate.

When he entered the yard and approached the house, Ellie came running out of the front door. She wore her good blue dress and her hair lay smooth on her shoulders. "Rafe, I heard a shot about three hours after you left. I thought you might be bringing home a deer."

Rafe looked up to smile at the guilty look on her face. "You didn't hear my rifle, Honey. Somebody put a fifty caliber slug right through Lin Richardson's chest. Killed him deader'n two cents. The sheriff and I sure couldn't figure out what he was doing down here on Taylor's creek, though."

Steadying herself with one hand against the porch post Ellie stared down at Rafe's blank expression as she whispered, "Oh, my God. No."

Her face went white as realization jumped into her eyes. She sat down on the step. Her voice trembled as she whispered, "You did it, didn't you Rafe?"

Rafe leaned his rifle against the steps. "I don't know what in thunder you're raving about, woman. Go get my supper. I'm going to feed the stock."

The Touch of Love

Jennie

Tom looked down at the street before he pulled the shade. People were crowding along the sidewalk, going home from work. Some carried packages and brown sacks.

No one looked up. He was invisible there in the window. He slid the window down and pulled the green shade carefully so it wouldn't snap back.

He couldn't stand the noise when it snapped back. It was an ugly, stupid noise. He pushed his pale hair back out of his eyes as he turned around. With a strained, slow motion movement, he went into the bedroom and turned on the light.

It had grown dark while he remembered. Jennie always tried to stop him from remembering. She'd laugh and tell him things that happened at school. She'd tell about Bill and Wayland fighting over Ruth and other silly things.

Jennie was still lying on the blue rug. Tom smiled as he reached over and pulled her skirt over her knees. Her face was quiet. She had stopped crying and yelling.

He knelt at her side and whispered. "She is so beautiful. She has always been too beautiful."

Her blue eyes were looking at him. He slipped his arms under her and lifted her, held her close for a moment, then placed her on the bed.

He'd put clean sheets and the flowered quilt Jennie's mom made on the bed so it would look neat and pretty. Jennie always wanted things neat and pretty.

"It makes you feel better." She would say.

He straightened her arms and legs and pulled her clothes in place. The marks showed on her neck, dark smudgy, blue spots on each side. He touched them gently, watching his fingers, feeling the smoothness of her skin.

Tom started remembering again. Remembering how much he needed Jennie. She made him feel real. People came to see him when she was there. They laughed and talked - comfortable because she made people feel that way.

When she ran up the stairs and came in the apartment she always called to him. "Tom, Tom, are you here?"

He was always there before she came home. Sometimes she brought bread and vegetables in a brown sack so she could fix supper.

Tom shook himself awake. He had to keep going, to get Jennie ready before Bill and Wayland came.

Jennie was going to fix spaghetti and they were going to play cards. They always played cards on Friday night. He rummaged in Jennie's suitcase for her red scarf and put it around her neck. Lifting her head carefully, he slid the scarf under her neck and left it loose so it wouldn't hurt her. She looked nice with the red against her dark hair and white skin.

Tom unpacked Jennie's suitcase and placed her things back in the dresser and closet the way she liked them and put the suitcase back under the bed.

"Don't worry, Jennie. I'll have everything ready. It won't take me any time to cook the spaghetti. I know just what to put in it."

The room was clean and everything looked right again. Tom clicked off the light so it wouldn't shine in Jennie's eyes.

He went into the kitchen, humming to himself, and put the canned sauce and noodles on to cook.

The doorknob rattled and someone pounded on the panels. Tom ran through the living room and opened the door. Bill and Wayland walked past him into the room.

"What the hell is the door locked for?" asked Bill. "We thought maybe you love birds forgot it was Friday."

Tom watched Bill as he snickered and looked at Wayland knowingly. He felt the cold hate creeping up in him.

"Come on in, I'm tending supper." He led the way into the kitchen. Both men leaned against the cabinets.

Bill said, "What are you doing K.P. for Tom? Where's Jennie?"

"She's lying down. We'll go in and see her in a minute."

"What's wrong with her? She's not sick?" Wayland stood up straight, looking worried.

"No, of course she's not sick. Did you ever know Jennie to get sick? Come on, we can go while the spaghetti cooks." Tom pulled the towel from around his waist and led the way to the bedroom.

"She's beautiful lying there so quiet, isn't she?" Tom reached over and stroked Jennie's cheek.

"Tom, for God's sake, what's wrong with her?" Wayland's voice was hoarse. Bill's face was ashen.

"Nothing's wrong with her. What could be wrong?' Tom glared at the two men. "She's resting until supper is ready, that's all."

"Wayland looked at Bill, "What's wrong with her, Bill?"

"Shut up." Bill's words were clipped and harsh. He went over and placed a restraining hand on Wayland's arm.

"Tom, he said, Wayland and I can't stay. We just came by to tell you we can't have supper tonight.

"I've got to get on back home. Dad needs me to help him work on his truck tonight."

"You can't stay? But, we always play cards on Friday night."

"We'll come back another night, another time. Bill was backing out the door. "Come on Wayland."

Tom went back into the kitchen and finished preparing the meal. He fixed his plate and stood in the middle of the floor to eat. "No use messing up the table for one," he thought.

Tom slept on the couch again. His back and legs felt stiff as a board. The sun was bright outside when he peeped around the shade.

He started at the sound of footsteps in the hall. Mrs. King, he thought. That old bitch will want to come in. He tiptoed to the door and shot the bolt. The footsteps went on down the hall.

He signed with relief. "It's another week before the rent is due, anyway."

Tom pulled on his jeans and buttoned his shirt up to the neck. He liked his neck covered. He went in the bedroom.

Jennie's eyes were closed now. Her face was beginning to look funny. Tom slipped his finger under the red scarf. It was too tight. He re-tied it and sat beside Jennie trying to think.

A soft, sweet smell filled the room. Jennie never wore perfume. She knew he hated it. His nose was itching. Tom went into the living room and paced up and down. The room was looking shabby.

He went into the kitchen and opened the refrigerator. Everything was running out. He'd have to go out again.

Tom put on his shoes and looked in Jennie's pocketbook for some money. He locked the dead bolt when he went out. Mrs. King didn't have a key to that.

He stopped in the hallway and looked at the mailbox. There'd be two letters from Jennie's father now. He wrote to her every week. Jennie always wrote back the next day.

The sun burned Tom's eyes. He took out his dark glasses and put them on, feeling safer. He went on to the store. As he turned the corner on the way back to the apartment he saw Ruth go into his apartment building.

"Oh, no." He muttered, "She'll talk forever."

Tom stepped back around the corner and waited until Ruth came back out of the building and went to her car. He watched as she pulled away, then rushed up to the apartment and bolted the door after him.

The smell was everywhere now. The headache was back and his nose itched again. It made his throat hurt. He went in the bedroom and covered Jennie with the extra blanket, tucking it over her head to hide her blotchy face.

"I should have let Ruth come in," Tom thought. "She loves Jennie. She would know what to do."

Tom pulled his suitcase out from under the bed and packed his things. It didn't take long. He'd have to go stay with someone for a few days. He hated to go home. Mom would ask questions.

He ran his hand over his hair and realized it was dirty. He'd have to take a shower. Jennie hated for him to get dirty. He stood under the shower for a long time, then dried on one of Jennie's pink towels. He put on his good trousers and a white shirt then picked up his suitcase and started through the living room.

Someone knocked on the door. "Who is it?" he called.

"It's Ruth, Tom. Can I come in?"

"Just a minute," he said. Tom opened the door a crack and peeped out. A policeman stood behind Ruth.

"I came to see Jennie, Tom. Bill and Wayland said there was something wrong with her."

Tom stared at Ruth for a long moment trying to decide what to do. His nose started itching again.

"She's right here in the bedroom, Ruth. Come on in.

Goodbye

My Friend

Uncle Willie always called me "Boy." He knew I was a girl all right, but he also knew I hated being treated different, like I was some kind of freak or something the men didn't know how to react to.

Uncle Willie kind of shuffled when he walked. He must have been awfully old. I thought about fifty or even more.

His clothes were old too. They even had a kind of odd smell, like old things get. His hair was white, and his skin was a nice, soft brown. I thought it looked right funny.

He and Aunt Lizzie lived in the old-school house in the back of our yard. He worked the tobacco on shares with Daddy and Aunt Lizzie helped Mama in the house.

I was fascinated by outdoor things. I wanted to know why leaves got green and seeds made the right kind of plants grow and why cows sometimes had two calves.

I guess Uncle Willie thought I needed his help. I heard him say "poor child" under his breath many a time just before he carefully explained to me things like "skunks stinks because God made them so, Boy. They fits God's plan and that's all there is to it."

Well, you can bet I couldn't let that rest. I worried that poor old man continuously. He never lost patience, though. He'd take my hand in his huge fist and walk along telling me how God made grass thin and pointy for a purpose and that flies were useful creatures or God wouldn't have sent them to us.

Uncle Willie cried when I went away to school. I remember thinking how silly old men could be.

He made me a wide belt out of the skin of a big black snake he killed beside the shed. I thanked him properly and packed it in my suitcase. I had to keep that thing hidden in my clothes all term. You couldn't give girls a chance to get something like that to tease you about. Just being from the country was bad enough.

I did real well in school at first. I was way ahead in reading. Daddy taught me the words in the funny papers when I was a baby. I felt like I could always read. But algebra got me. Whoever dreamed up that stuff was getting back at the whole human race for some disgraceful thing somebody did. I'm sure Uncle Willie would have attributed the ridiculous stuff to God's plan, But I felt sure God couldn't be that silly.

I felt real again on holidays and summer vacation. At first Uncle Willie met me at the store with the wagon when I got off the train. We'd pick up right where we left off. Me forever asking questions and him explaining God's hand in making things work like they ought to.

One summer, Daddy bought a car. Its workings forever stayed a mystery to Uncle Willie. After that someone else from the farm met me.

I tried to find time to talk things over with Uncle Willie, but Mama was forever telling me "get on your new white dress and hurry." She drug me around to visit her friends and shop until I was sick to death of it.

I tried to balk on her, but Daddy turned against me. He put on his "Father" voice and said, "Honey, you're a young lady now. Do as your mother says."

Botheration! Being a young lady was the dumbest thing. You had to stay clean and wear a dress and keep your hair straight. You couldn't run or cuss or anything.

The summer I was thirteen, I saw that Uncle Willie was really getting old and feeble. Aunt Lizzie had passed away the year before.

He didn't work the tobacco any more. He just spent most of his time sitting on his step and smoking. I used to slip out to pass the time of day, but about as soon as I got out a "How are you" Mama would scream and I'd have to go back to the house.

I didn't write to Uncle Willie when I was away at school. He couldn't read words. That didn't mean he was dumb. Lots of old colored folks couldn't read books or papers or letters. He could read the weather and tracks and people, best of anyone I've ever known.

Besides, Mama would have had to read my letter to him, and I just couldn't do that.

When I was ready to leave for school that fall Uncle Willie hobbled out to the front yard and stood by the car while I was packing my things in. He waited until right before I left before he said a word. The he said, "you be good, Little Missy"

When I came home for the Christmas holiday Mama told me. We were sitting at the supper table. "Poor Old Uncle Willie passed away last month." She said. "He took a cold and it settled in his lungs. I guess he was just too old to fight it."

I sat still and looked at her, working to keep my face quiet. Daddy reached over and held my hand under the table.

A New Ending

A Can of Corned Beef

My hands trembled as I fumbled with my keys. I finally got the door open and slipped into the safety of my apartment. Dropping my shopping bag on the floor I leaned back against the door panels to catch my breath.

I always react that way. I'll never get used to it.

I flopped down in my chair and pulled off my hat. My heart was still pounding from rushing up so many steps.

I know I'm getting too old for such excitement. There's no other way, though. I will not give up. I refuse to sit here and slowly starve, and I'm not going to live with my daughter and her nasty-nice lump of a husband.

The apartment is getting so shabby, it's really a disgrace. I've got stacks of books and magazines in every corner. I guess it's none to clean either, but I don't really care about that. Hell, the dirt will out-live me, that's for sure.

Joyce can keep her house sterilized if that's the way she wants it. I couldn't feel comfortable for a minute in that place. Her jerk of a husband would put my old books out in his garage for sure, if he didn't make me throw them away or try to sell them.

My feet are killing me. These shoes are so old they could draw social security. They'd probably get about as big a check as I do. I really should try to find me some new ones. You're always supposed to take care of your feet. Oh, well. First things first.

I guess I'd better push myself up out of this chair and take my "shopping" to the kitchen. As cramped as this refrigerator is, my piddling bit of groceries look lost on the shelf. Seven dollars and eighty cents gone and all I got was potatoes, onions, cottage cheese, a cabbage that needs throwing away and one pack of cigarettes.

I know I ought to quit smoking. Joyce is always saying--'Mama, you'll kill yourself.' Her resident son-of-a-bitch won't let me smoke in his perfect house. I'm not going to worry about it. If over sixty years of smoking hasn't killed me, I think I'm safe.

The extra things are in the bottom of the bag. I got two cans of potted ham and a small jar of coffee. I wish sugar were packed in something small enough. I used to drink my coffee black all the time, but I was just vain and watching my weight. A little fat would do me good now.

I love sugar in my coffee. Two or three big spoons full.

It's hard to think about how bad things were for almost a year after Donald died. I went without eating anything some days until I learned how to manage.

My social security check is so doggone small it's gone before I can take a deep breath, but Martha Carey taught me how to make it stretch.

Martha invited me to a card party at her apartment. She served smoked salmon, liver pate, and real shrimp. I couldn't believe my eyes. I guess she noticed how much I ate, because she asked me to stay a few minutes after the other women left.

Martha made us a cup of tea with sugar and real cream. We sat at her kitchen table to drink it. She came right to the point.

"Listen to me Belle." She had a real determined look in her blue eyes. "You don't have enough money to eat right, do you?"

I was too astonished to be embarrassed. I just stared at her. She reached over and put her hand on mine.

"Don't look at me like that, dear. We've been friends for too many years. I've found a way to get by and I'm going to tell you about it. Now, don't you interrupt me until I finish and don't reject what I tell you until you've thought about it long and hard."

She told me then. I was flabbergasted. Martha Carey of all people. I left her apartment and walked back here in sort of a daze.

At first, I tried to put it out of my mind—tried to pretend I never heard what she said, but about the twentieth of the month I was down to beans and potatoes again--no onions, no sugar, and smoking my last pack of cigarettes.

I stopped trying to rationalize and just did it. I went to the new A&P store and bought a loaf of bread and stole a can of corned beef.

It's still hard for me. I'm surprised I don't get caught. I know I must show how terrified I am in way I move. By the time I get back here to the apartment I'm almost sick.

I'd better go write down where I shopped today and what I wore before I forget. Tomorrow I'm going to try the new Safeway on Marshall Street. I'll wear my old blue jacket and no hat.

I don't think anyone ever looks at my face anymore, anyway.

Anne Haw Holt

Anne Haw Holt, writing as A. H. Holt, is a Virginian transplanted to a 1910 "Cracker" cottage in Monticello, Florida. She attended PVCC in Charlottesville, Va. and received her BA from Mary Baldwin in Staunton, VA in 1989. She holds a MA and Ph.D. in History from Florida State University in Tallahassee, Florida.

Anne is an accomplished storyteller and photographer. She writes fiction, poetry, and non-fiction on writing, history, parenting and Frontier Florida. Dr. Holt writes grants and teaches writing, grant writing, writing and leadership.

Other Books By
A. H. Holt

Fiction

High Plains Fort
Ten in Texas
Silver Creek
Blanco Sol
Riding Fence
Kendrick
Blood Redemption
XIT Ranch
The Malefactors

Nonfiction

Grant Writing Step by Step
From Writer to Author
Beautiful Places:
Monticello & Jefferson County Florida

Introducing The Malefactors, an epic story set in Biblical times about the lives of the thieves that where crucified with Jesus Christ.

Based on a story originally written by Anne's father *Richardson Wallace Haw, Jr.*

Anne has outdone herself with The Malefactors. I couldn't put it down. A character driven marvelous story.

The Malefactors

By
Anne Haw Holt &
Richardson Wallace Haw, Jr.

Preface

Josias' head sagged, his chin almost touching his chest. The pain had stopped. He could no longer feel his hands and feet, but his chest hurt -- he could hardly breathe. Hours passed. Occasionally, as from a distance, he heard Lucius' bitter voice, cursing and railing against his fate.

Forcing his eyes open, he squinted against the hot sun. Most of the crowds were gone. Several groups of people knelt or sat on the sand at the bottom of the hill. The soldiers allowed only a few to climb close to the crosses. Two women sat together near the brow of the hill. Forcing his eyes to focus, Josias recognized the scarf his mother wore and the tendrils of dark hair touching Sarah's brow.

Sarah, oh Sarah, my beloved wife.

He closed his eyes on the tears that blinded him and slipped into unconsciousness. Hours later he awakened again. There was no sound from Lucius. Straining, Josias finally opened his eyes a little way. The sun was gone. The cool night of the desert was falling. The two women still sat on the sand.

I wonder if they're thirsty—if they will soon leave—they should go home. They know they should not be here alone. They should find Barabbas--he will protect them. I did not see Barabbas. He wasn't here—he should have been here—Argubus should have been here—.

Chapter 1

The hot, high sun of late afternoon beat relentlessly against the craggy rock cliffs overlooking the empty Roman road west of Jerusalem. Argubus the cripple seemed barely alive. He lay snuggled into a niche under a wide-overhanging cliff, high above the north side of the highway.

Many, many hours the old man spent sitting quietly, watching the road below, ever on the lookout for travelers. His lot, among the many followers of Barabbas, was to watch for some victim for the small robber band hiding in the bush filled wadi below. It was a trying, tiresome task, but one that him paid well. For Barabbas was generous in the division of spoils.

As he lay half-dozing in him as Argubus the Prophet. He the hot shade, Argubus' thoughts were of the clever ways of his life. In the teeming city, people knew forever warned anyone who would stop to listen to his tirades of the anger God felt for his chosen people. They committed many sins.

Most mornings found him at the entrance of David Street. He marched up and down before the gate, waved his arms about and loudly prophesied the forth-coming curses that would soon be visited upon all Jewry by a vengeful God. He told his listeners of a God angered with his people for collaborating with the Romans—for allowing graven images to be displayed in the Holy City and for their many, many sins.

After his harangue, Argubus would go through the crowd holding out his beggar's cup, seeking coins—coins he loudly proclaimed he would use to help the poor. He stared into the face of each person, a wild look of madness in his yellowish-brown eyes. The grim and fearsome expression on his sun-darkened face intimidated many out of at least one small coin.

When he gathered sufficient contributions, he would then leave the city, announcing to everyone in hearing distance that he was going into the desert to commune with God. He promised he would return the next morning to reveal his message to the people. Many scoffed at the old man's preaching of doom, yet others believed and were fearful.

Argubus chuckled to himself as he thought of the foolishness of the devout. Especially those who believed him and gave of their small possessions, for he was a wealthy man according to the standards of his followers. He thought gleefully of a small hoard of coins hidden in a rock cleft directly behind where he sat. It was only a small sample of his treasure. He started to reach for the coins, to know the joy of holding their round smoothness in his hands, when out of the corner of his eye he saw a small dust cloud rising far up the road.

Keeping his head down, he crawled to the far side of the overhanging rocks. Staying bent close to the ground, he scurried down the steep path to the ravine behind the cliffs.

"Josias, Josias, hurry to the lookout and see who comes."

Alarmed and excited, every member of the waiting band dropped what they were doing and rushed to gather around the old man. He waved one arm toward the lookout post.

"Go and see for yourselves."

Josias, leader of the band and Emilack, the youngest member, rushed to climb the cliff path to the spot overlooking the road. Josias pushed his long hair away from his face and held one hand over his eyes to shade them as he cautiously peered over the rocks. The caravan was hidden from his view by a bend in the road. He motioned for Emilack to drop down lower in the rocks to assure he could not be seen.

The two men chafed at the long wait. Finally, the approaching caravan came near enough so they could examine it. Made up of a string of pack asses following a richly dressed merchant, the train moved slowly. The man rode on a fat black mule with richly caparisoned harness. Six poorly armed guards marched on each side of the merchant. The men moved dispiritedly, as though they were exhausted from a long day's march.

Josias crowed with delight as he turned to Emilack. "Look, my friend. The caravan will be rich. Watch the way the guards walk—they're exhausted. They'll be no threat to us and there are no soldiers within miles. This could turn out to be an afternoon well spent."

Still keeping their heads low, he and Emilack rushed back down the path to the waiting men. Motioning for them to come close so he would not have to shout, Josias ordered, "You men see to your weapons and get mounted. We're going to take that caravan. It looks as if it was made for us."

After a great scurrying about, Josias and ten well-armed men mounted their small but sturdy horses and rode to the narrow pass west of camp. Argubus returned to his lookout—he knew his part well. The robber crew hid themselves in the rocks and brush and waited impatiently for the old man's signal to attack.

Argubus looked up and down the road again, to make sure no Roman Patrol rode within sight. As the caravan came abreast of the opening of the wadi that hid Josias' band, the old man screamed the signal to attack. The men swept down on the caravan guards, scimitars swinging. It was over in no more than an instant and the tired guards were dead.

Josias himself held the merchant with his sword point in his throat. He ordered his men to clear the road of all evidence of the raid. Working in tandem, the men dragged the bodies of the slain guards into the broken rocks and brush and tipped them over into the ravine.

When the bodies lay all piled together, Josias' men broke the rim of the ravine and pushed dirt over the dead guards. Finally, the robbers lead their own horses and the heavily laden mules through the mouth of the wadi and out of sight of the road.

Simon of Cyrenia sat his mount quietly, watching the eyes of the robber who still held his sword at his throat. Other members of the man's band rummaged through his merchandise. His chest swelled with anger to know that the robbers touched his possessions, but he was cautious. Wisely reasoning that if the robbers planned to kill him he would already lie dead, he kept silent. All he could do was wait and see what would happen.

Tired of the golden-haired bandit grinning at him, Simon finally said, "I shall inform Rome of Pilate's inability to make his province safe for honest merchants."

"And well you may someday, my fine merchant," Josias said, smiling at the anger so plain to hear in Simon's voice. "If it happens that our master sees fit to hold you for ransom instead of taking your life."

Simon of Cyrenia was one of the most successful traveling merchants in the Empire. He began his work young and seemed naturally shrewd to all those who dealt with him. Many named him a worthy descendant of Phoenician traders.

Usually he gathered costly items along the Southern Mediterranean Sea, conveyed them across the old Syrian caravan routes to Damascus and from there took them to Antioch and Corinth. He sold these goods to the wealthiest residents of those cities. Men and women demanded the best of the Empire's offerings. Everything Simon offered his customers was of great value. The robbers shouted with joy as they opened the packs and examined their loot.

When it was full dark and safe, the men set out on a familiar path, leading the laden animals around the city to Gihon. From that place they could smuggle goods into Jerusalem by a secret door in the side of Nehemiah's tunnel.

Moving everything in the packs took many trips by all members of the band that could be spared from guard duty. Carrying the heavy packs on their shoulders, the men splashed their way through the cold waters that flowed under the city's walls. As soon as the merchandise all lay safely hidden away, Josias turned Simon over to two of his most trusted men.

"Take this merchant to the hidden valley, Micah. You and Elias stay there to guard him. Keep careful watch as you turn west of Mount Guarantania and Jericho. There will surely be Roman patrols moving about in that area. Take care you do not ride into them. This man will bring us a rich ransom.

"Don't you dare forget to blindfold him when you get close to the mountain. He appears sharp and will probably remember everything he sees on the way. It wouldn't do for him to remember the road to our valley."

Barabbas watched Josias' face as he recounted step by step every minute of the successful raid and described the valuable merchandise the men hid in their secret place. The bandit leader tried to keep a scowl on his leathered face, but could not contain an occasional grin. He was undeniably pleased with the returns from the attack on Simon the Cyrenian's caravan.

He felt dismay however, when he learned that Josias decided to hold the merchant for ransom. It was Barabbas' policy to kill everyone in a caravan. That policy served him well and kept his band in safety for many years. Only Josias dared to resort to holding his victims for ransom.

"You will let your greed for gold be our downfall, man. You're a fool to hold men captive instead of killing them." Barabbas began to shout angrily to Josias as soon as he rode into the hidden camp.

Josias showed no fear of Barabbas. Dismounting, he dropped the reins of his horse and approached the bandit chief. "Master, please listen to me. This is a truly wealthy merchant. He is far different from the usual petty traveling peddlers we find. His family will pay well for his release."

"Yes, I suppose they will at that. But what of the day you hold a friend of Caesar or another official of the empire?"

Grinning impudently, Josias said, "That time Master, may be the day we have our fill of excitement."

Barabbas stared at Josias thoughtfully. He valued the man greatly, but feared that his shrewdness and lack of fear would someday take him too far. He could endanger the entire band.

"Meet me at the summit beyond Rimmon at dark tomorrow. We will ride to the valley and see this merchant. I, Barabbas, shall decide his fate."

A little after moonrise the next night, Josias and Barabbas heard the challenge of a guard as they made their cautious way along a steep, rocky defile afoot, leading their horses.

"Halt where you are."

"It is I, Barabbas, and one of my captains."

"Enter Master, and peace be unto you."

A small fire guided their way to a cave-like shelter. The opening was hollowed out from the limestone cliff by some ancient river. All the men of the band except the guard at the narrow entrance and one other man slept beyond the fire, rolled in their blankets.

Without a word of greeting to the man beside the fire Barabbas announced, "We will sleep the night out here, and tomorrow I will talk to the prisoner." Taking his own blanket from the back of his mount, he joined the men who lay around the fire and soon fell asleep.

There was a great stir in the camp when the men wakened and realized Barabbas joined them in the night. Lucius, the captain of the band, feared the bandit chief's visit. His band had found little luck in the last few weeks. He felt tremendous relief when after breakfast Barabbas covered his face with a scarf and called for Josias' prisoner to be brought before him. Lucius' heart swelled with pleasure when he noticed the serious look on Barabbas face.

I hope he's so angry with that Josias he kills him as an example—right here before my men. If he does it here, it will make the cowards even more afraid not to obey my orders.

Following a guard, the prisoner emerged from an adjacent cave to stand before Barabbas. Turning to Josias and speaking pleasantly, Barabbas said, "Tell me about this fine prisoner we have here."

"He calls himself Simon of Cyrene, Master. He is surely a merchant of great importance."

"Is this so?" Barabbas said, laughing a little. "We shall see. Were his possessions many, my friend?"

"Yes, his goods are on their way to the usual place to be sold. I am convinced they will bring a tremendous price. Here is a heavy pouch of gold I realized from selling the fine animals of his caravan."

Pulling a rolled sheepskin from a fold in his robe Barabbas said, "Good, let us write a demand to his steward for ransom. Here, use this fine sheepskin. To what relative shall we send our ransom demand, Simon of Cyrene?"

Simon's voice trembled with anger. He held himself proudly, and stared into Josias' eyes, "Write it to my son, James of Cyrene."

"You will be pleased at the high value we set upon you Simon of Cyrene." Barabbas turned to Josias, saying, "Captain, write the ransom for five hundred shekels." He laughed aloud when he turned back and saw the expression of smoldering anger on Simon's face.

Barabbas handed Simon his own business seal, stolen from the merchant's personal possessions. "Here Merchant," Barabbas said, "Stamp the demand at the bottom with this, so it will be recognized by your son."

When Simon finished placing his seal on the document and handed it back to Barabbas, the bandit chief asked, amusement apparent in his voice, "Are you sure your son will think you worth such a sum?"

Simon turned away, pretending interest in the fire and refused to respond to the man's crude humor.

Rolling the piece of skin tightly and tying it with a strip of rag, Barabbas summoned one of his men. "You will take this message to Cyrene. There you will find the house of Simon and give this to his son's hand. The man you seek is known as James."

Leaning forward, he stared into the man's eyes. "Do not fail me. If you do you know I will punish you and all those you love. Remember what I say, I know where your family lives."

Without another word, Barabbas stepped to the other side of the fire. Still masked, he confronted Lucius. "I am disappointed in you and your men, my friend. I will give you only a few more weeks to do your part."

He turned away from Lucius without waiting for an answer and joined Josias at the horses. The two men immediately set out for Jerusalem, leaving Simon of Cyrene to wait in captivity for the many months it would take the messenger to deliver the message and return with the ransom.

The eastern band of Barabbas' men, under control of Barsubus the Philistine, known to his men as Lucius the Hawk, because of his prominent nose and vicious ways, operated along the old King's Highway in Perea. This was a vast, thinly populated area of wild and desolate country. There were many places to hide and escape if chased by the Roman Legion. The country, filled with rocks and gorges, contributed more to the band's success than the wisdom of their leader, for although Lucius was noted for his savagery, he did not have the cunning of Josias.

After Barabbas and Josias left the camp, Lucius sat in the shade of an acacia tree, nursing his jealous anger over Josias' success. "He's got the best place to operate. Old Argubus advised it. Damn both of them any way.

"I'll show them, I'll pull the biggest robbery ever heard of, bigger than Josias ever dreamed. Salem has gone to Gadara to watch for the next large caravan coming in this direction. He'll have plenty of time to ride ahead and warn us so we can get set.

"We'll give Barabbas something to brag about of us. It will be a relief to stop him always talking of the exploits of that infernal Josias and his men."

Lucius' very jaws ached when he thought of the insult he suffered when Barabbas chided him for his poor showing with his men looking on.

Josias and Argubus throw it up to me every time I see them. That Josias might not brag much, but he has a lofty air. He walks around with his head up in the air as though he thinks he's better than anyone else—that's worse yet—I'll find a way to get even with him someday.

Far into the night Lucius schemed and plotted future deeds. He planned how he would execute the biggest robbery the Empire ever experienced. It would be so big it would bring out a whole legion from Rome. Then he, Lucius the Hawk, bandit leader, would have followers of his own. He would be able to get out from under the heavy thumb of Barabbas.

Lucius schemed on, completely unaware of his shortcomings. He never knew that Barabbas only kept him around because of his murderous ferocity. His activities often kept Pilate's Legion searching the hills east of Jerusalem, leaving the road between Joppa and Jerusalem clear and enabling Josias to overcome many travelers.

It chafed Lucius greatly that he must await Barabbas' orders as to what caravan he might raid, and what merchant he might attack. He shook his head in bitterness as he thought of the ignominy. He could feel the shame in his gut, pressing, pressing against him.

Attack this one, it is poorly guarded. Do not attack that one--that one is a favorite of Rome or do not dare touch this other one, or this man is owed a favor. He did not need this rigid control, he could decide for himself. He could decide just as the upstart Josias did— and he would do it soon.

The headquarters of Lucius' band lay well hidden in the foothills east of the Jordan River. The camp was in a small clearing amidst a jumble of rocks, locust trees and wild grapevines. It gave the band almost impenetrable cover. A spring furnished unlimited sweet water and some small caves in the stone wall more than filled the need for shelter during falling weather.

A merciless leader, the men of the band and their women feared Lucius' unpredictability. Oftentimes he got the idea that one of his men may have complained to Barabbas of his cruelty. The thought didn't bother him overmuch. He knew Barabbas had grown soft and would have little heart if it ever came to a fight between them. Lucius believed he would easily kill the bandit chief in hand to hand combat.

Late one morning, after dreaming into the night how he would glorify himself, Lucius was awakened by the high sun reflected on mica flecks in stones at the cave's entrance. It was much later in the day than he usually rose.

Throwing aside his blankets and moving closer to the small campfire, Lucius chuckled as the women scurried to prepare his breakfast, thinking he was still in the bad mood of the previous night. He looked around the camp. Men were posted at the valley entrance and atop a high pinnacle of rock. Without instruction, they watched the road.

"Are there travelers on the road?" he cupped his hands around his mouth and shouted to the man on lookout.

"I see no one, Master."

The man's answer greatly amused Lucius. He required his men to call him master whenever Barabbas wasn't about to hear them. It helped somewhat to overcome his feeling of inferiority to the man who owned him, for Lucius was a slave.

Early in the afternoon, one of the lookouts rode into the camp with news of a large caravan heading to Jerusalem from Damascus. He described the caravan as well laden with goods and heavily guarded.

Jumping up to face the man, Lucius shouted, "Did you count the guards?"

"Yes Master—I counted twelve. They were well armed with spears and swords. Each of them carry one of those huge Damascus shields."

"Were they mounted?"

"No Master, they are not. Only the merchant was mounted. He rides like a Samaritan. Two guards walked ahead of the caravan and the rest followed behind. Those men drove twenty heavily-laden pack asses before them."

Turning to his men, Lucius raised his voice to say, "Prepare for an attack at first light. I will ride ahead and spy out their camp."

Salem, the lookout that brought the message, stepped out of Lucius' reach and spoke softly, "Master, it would be better for us to ride now and attack as they make camp. Those guards are all tired to exhaustion from their long march. We would have a great advantage over them. Also, we would have the entire night to escape."

"You would give orders as Barabbas?" Lucius jerked around to face the man, yelling in his anger and astonishment at such temerity.

Cringing farther away, Salem said nothing more. He hurried to join the men who were busily stuffing food into their saddlebags. When they finished they brought the hobbled horses closer to camp, and made ready to ride. There was none of the normal jesting and laughter. Few of the men relished the idea of attacking so strong a force.

It took only a few minutes for the men to lead their horses away from the camp far enough to reach a flat area. Once the reached the plain and all were mounted, they spurred their horses to a gallop and headed for a hill several miles to the west.

When he reached the brow of the hill, Salem held his hand high, signaling for the men behind him to stop. Stretching out his arm, he pointed to the group of animals, off to the side of the roadway. A large fire revealed the outline of men huddled close together partly within the circle of light. Another, smaller fire glowed nearby. It undoubtedly provided warmth for the merchant.

Without dismounting, Lucius leaned forward to speak softly, "Withdraw out of sight in that hollow to the right. That's well out of sight of the merchant's camp. We can't risk a fire. Even if they didn't see it, they would smell it. You can sit close together to keep warm. Get some sleep if you can, and be ready to attack at first light.

"I'm going to check the area and make ready for a surprise attack at dawn."

The men sat huddled together in the darkness of their hiding place, glumly muttering about "lambs led to the slaughter."

Raising his head, Salem spoke softly, but loud enough for all to hear, "Surely Lucius is demented. He is planning for us to attack a caravan with more guards than he has followers."

"I wonder about him of late," Aaron of Judah muttered, "He has done some strange things since we were sent here from the Joppa road."

A deep voice from the shadows said, "We were only sent here because Barabbas trusts Josias more that he does Lucius."

"Shh—keep your voice down—he comes." Salem cautioned.

Lucius dismounted and thrust the reins of his horse to the nearest man without looking at him. In a harsh whisper, he demanded, "Are all of your weapons sharpened? Have you checked your shield bucklers? You know a loose buckler can cost you your life—check them now—all of you."

"All is in readiness, Master." One of the men answered for the group.

In the semi-dark and cold of the early morning, ten reluctant highwaymen mounted their horses to follow Lucius as he rode over the hill and onto the sandy edge of the highway. Holding their animals in to move quietly, they headed for the camp of the Samaritan.

Lucius, overbold and dreaming of his forthcoming triumph, allowed his horse to wander from the sandy roadside onto the main track. The animal's shod hooves struck the stones of the road. The sharp sound awakened one of the soldiers who guarded the camp.

The man jumped up and screamed a warning to the rest of the guards as he grabbed for his weapons. "We're attacked. Prepare to defend the camp."

All surprise was lost. Lucius spurred his horse over the rocks and into the camp shouting for his men to attack.

"Kill them, kill them all."

His men, lacking confidence from the start, followed him to the edge of the camp, but once there, most of them turned aside, urging their horses into the rocks and trees away from the road, desperate to escape what appeared to be certain death. A tall Syrian slammed the side of his spear against Lucius' head, unhorsing him.

Much later, Lucius stirred and tried to move. His head hurt as if it would split. His arms were bound behind his back. The shaft of a broken spear passed though the bend of his elbows. Groaning, he opened his eyes. Three of his men lay dead. Their bodies still sprawling where they fell. He could see no other prisoners.

Bitterly, he swore to himself. "The rest of the cowards ran away."

The tall Syrian, evidently the leader of the guards, was shouting at the merchant. "Let us kill the vicious scum and have done with it. That will surely be his fate if we take him to Jerusalem."

"No," the white bearded Samaritan ordered in a soft but stern voice. "That is the way of the ungodly. We will turn him over to Pilate's jailers when we reach Jerusalem. If there will be blood shed let it be on their hands."

"It would be better to kill him now."

The old man still shook his head. "No. I'll hear no more of it."

Much to the disgust of the guards he ordered, "Get shovels, you men. We'll bury these souls here."

The merchant stood by until the three dead highwaymen were well covered in a common grave. He added greatly to the chagrin of the guards by bowing his head to say some sort of prayer to his strange god.

The Syrians muttered among themselves about the strangeness of Jews. The tall guard said to the others, "They're always praying to some god men cannot see—a spirit they call their Lord. I'm convinced they are fools—they're all fools."

That night, the caravan camped near another that traveled north, in a smooth flat area hard by the sweet wells of Jericho. Still bound, Lucius leaned against the rough trunk of a palm tree, unable to sleep for the torture of the tight ropes and the hard spear shaft pulling against his back.

"Shh--." A voice whispered close behind him.

Lucius felt a hand on his bare forearm. Almost immediately, he heard the whisper of a sharp knife against the rope and his bonds fell away. His savior touched his arm again and motioned for him to follow. After crawling some distance away from the sleeping guards, his liberator rose and ran ahead of him. Lucius ran at the man's heels.

Soon the man stopped beside two saddled horses waiting in the dense blackness of a vineyard. Once mounted, he and Lucius whipped their horses so that they ran wildly between the rows of vines. Soon they emerged onto a deserted roadway and turned south to race through hidden paths. Finally, they reached the safety of the hideout, in the rocks west of Guarantania.

Obed, one of the newest and youngest of Lucius' followers, sat beside a small fire. The rest of the band sat in a group behind him, their heads hanging dolefully, refusing to meet Lucius' eyes.

Lucius said nothing, but his eyes and expression clearly expressed the disgust he felt for men who would desert him. Wordlessly, he leaned from the saddle to grab a sword and spear from the nearest man. Strapping the sword around his waist he looked over the men's heads and barked an order in a voice that dared anyone to disobey him, "Get ready to ride."

Turning his horse, he spurred away, leading the band west. After a series of long night marches they finally reached a remote hideout in the desolate hills west of Gennesaret in Galilee. Lucius was afraid of returning to Jerusalem. He knew the guards and Samaritan they attacked could give the Romans a good description of him and probably of several of his men.

He was even more afraid when he thought of the anger of Barabbas. He dreaded their next meeting. He knew Barabbas would rage over the abortive robbery attempt. He would be furious over the loss of men, and more than furious at Lucius' failure to gain control of the rich train. Lucius brooded; knowing his failure would do nothing but increase Barabbas' confidence in Josias.

He is Barabbas pet—the perfect Josias of Bethany—he will be even more the pet now. It is Barabbas fault. He should not have given me such cowards as followers. This was not my fault. We would have won the train if the fools had not run away. But I will be blamed— I know I will be blamed. Then he will think Josias is even more perfect.

Books by Anne Haw Holt, also writing as A. H. Holt.

Beautiful Places,
Monticello & Jefferson County Florida

ISBN: 978-0692793251
https://goo.gl/57efpN

Beautiful Places is a gentle reminiscence blended with the heartfelt musings of a woman blessed to have experienced them. It is a rediscovery of our southern heritage and a renewal of our fascination with the wonders of our ancient world. Dr. Holt's photographs delightfully recreate her experiences and adventures in the small town of Monticello, an eclectic town with a rich, but little known history nestled in the natural beauty of Jefferson County, Florida.

Blanco Sol

ASIN: B00AF9GKDC
ISBN-13: 978-1477814956
https://goo.gl/4RhMJw

King Sutherland is dead---at least that's what both friend and foe assume. The war ended almost a year ago, yet King was seriously wounded after the surrender, delaying his return home. Recently recovered, he is on his way back to Texas and the Blanco Sol ranch.

Blood Redemption

ASIN: B009PJIIF6
ISBN-13: 978-1477814970
https://goo.gl/BSPBFY

Cousins Red and Wes are bitter rivals--Wes the spoiled heir of the sprawling White Willow Ranch and Red the son of a humble rancher. In the heat of an argument, Wes is poised to murder an unconscious Red, but in a panic, kills the onlooking barkeep instead. Red awakens to find himself framed for Wes' crime and is quickly sentenced and sent off to Yuma.

From Writer To Author
Prepare your Manuscript for
Publication

ASIN: B00B78JA9G
ISBN-13: 978-1517432881
https://goo.gl/CIq5fK

A simple walk through on how to edit and present your finished manuscript to a publisher. A clear and simple guide to reach the final revision of your manuscript before submitting your work to an agent or publisher. How to create a query letter, a written pitch and a verbal pitch of your work. Created and tested by a published author and writing teacher. This book will put you at the desk with your agent or editor as she reads your manuscript eliminating the need of hiring an editor.

Grant Writing Step By Step
A Simple, straightforward guidebook
for getting the money you need.

ASIN: B013QCN3I4
ISBN-13: 978-1516847884
https://goo.gl/d3OMD9

Grant Writing Step By Step shows how to collect the information you need to apply for grants for any project. Following the method outlined in this book you will develop the confidence to find and apply for grants to pay for your goals.

High Plains Fort

ASIN: B01M34JT6P
ISBN: 978-1539980827
https://goo.gl/AijkVd

Riding west to find a new life for himself and his beloved Amelia, Justin faces murderers on the trail. In Bent's fort he finds friends, but also a traitor planning to take the fort with the help of the Comanche. Warned, he prepares the fort and its people for the attack.

Kendrick

ASIN: B00BSMR2NC
ISBN-13: 978-1477814949
https://goo.gl/4ny6Xb

Wayne Kendrick is suspicious. His best friend, Jim Carson, has suddenly disappeared, and Jim's claim has been taken over by The Blake Mining Company, which claims the land was abandoned.

When Wayne meets with Jim's family, he finds the reason for his friend's sudden disappearance: he has been kidnapped! Reading a ransom note that Jim's family has discovered, Wayne promises he'll bring Jim home safely, aware even as he makes the oath that if his friend isn't dead already, he will be once the ransom has been paid.

Riding Fence

ASIN: B00A2NCKU8
ISBN-13: 978-1477814963
http://goo.gl/rWhL9G

Andre Devereaux paid well for his brother's daughter to be kidnapped and killed so he could inherit the family estate, but she was still alive, caring for the little boy Devereaux had recently made an orphan. It was time to find them and carry out his unfinished business.

Silver Creek

ASIN: B01GKGO35U
ISBN-13: 978-1539939481
https://goo.gl/dG5G20

John Garrett is my image of a real cowboy, and my heroes are still cowboys. He's good with his gun and his fists, but doesn't fight except when forced. Smart, loyal and tough, John captures your heart, and the heart of "Andy" Blaine the heroine. Andrea is a bit of a tom-boy, but a beautiful, strong and true western woman. John gets involved in the war for water rights on Silver Creek and neighboring ranches because his father seems to be involved on the wrong side of the law. He and his father haven't spoken for six years, but John feels it his duty to try to clear his father's name.

Ten In Texas

ASIN: B01EDDUA7W
ASIN: B01IRLBNHM
ISBN-13: 978-1530756582

Camping overnight in a draw on the newly released lands of the old XIT Ranch, Will Gantry suddenly feels an odd and welcome sense of belonging. He becomes friends with Dan, a deputy-sheriff, a beautiful woman and a young boy. He begins to make solid plans for the future that include an old cowboy named Pete and the professor. Will decides his idea of wandering down to Old Mexico can wait - - maybe forever.

The XIT Ranch
How Texas Traded Land for a State House

ASIN: B06XZ2VTHP
ISBN-13: 978-1517432881
http://goo.gl/CvM2VI

"The acquisition of three million acres of rangeland in the Panhandle, the construction of a state capitol building, and the creation of the XIT Ranch is a big, fantastic story that could only happen in Texas.

Thank you for reading this book.
Please take the time to share
and leave a review.

www.ingramcontent.com/pod-product-compliance
Lightning Source LLC
Chambersburg PA
CBHW070635130626
46555CB00006B/2559